The Boy Who Wanted to Cook

Gloria Whelan & Illustrated by Steve Adams

DISCOVER
the WORLD

Tales of the World *from* Sleeping Bear Press

FRANCE

Sleeping Bear Press gratefully acknowledges and thanks Hélène Potter
for her assistance and review of the French vocabulary.

Sleeping Bear Press™

315 East Eisenhower Parkway, Suite 200
Ann Arbor, MI 48108
www.sleepingbearpress.com

© 2011 Sleeping Bear Press is an imprint of Gale,
a part of Cengage Learning.

10 9 8 7 6 5 4 3 2 1

Library of Congress Cataloging-in-Publication Data

Whelan, Gloria.
The boy who wanted to cook / written by Gloria Whelan ; illustrated by Steve Adams.
p. cm.
Summary: Ten-year-old Pierre dreams of being a chef at his parents' restaurant, La Bonne Vache,
in the south of France and is told he is too young, but when an important guest comes Pierre
sees a chance to prove himself. Includes notes about dining in France and a glossary.
ISBN 978-1-58536-534-0
[1. Cooks--Fiction. 2. Restaurants--Fiction. 3. Family life--France--Fiction. 4. France--Fiction.]
I. Adams, Steve, 1967- ill. II. Title.
PZ7.W5718Boy 2011
[E]--dc22
2010053801

Printed by China Translation & Printing Services Limited,
Guangdong Province, China. 1st printing. 04/2011

PARIS

FRANCE

TARN RIVER

In the south of France near the River Tarn is the little restaurant, *La Bonne Vache*. The Good Cow takes its name from its famous *boeuf à la mode*, a delicious beef stew. In the kitchen of the restaurant is ten-year-old Pierre. Pierre's father, Monsieur Valcourt who is both chef and *patron* of the restaurant, says, "Pierre, go and play with your friends."

"Go fishing," says Pierre's mother. Madame Valcourt bakes the pastries for the restaurant.

But Pierre wants to cook. He longs to be a great chef like his father and his grandfather before him.

Pierre's father tells him, "Pierre, you are too young to cook."

As Pierre rides his bicycle under the chestnut trees he imagines a chestnut *soufflé*. When he passes a wood he thinks of the little *morilles*, the tasty mushrooms that grow there.

A pair of goats look to him like a very large goat cheese. On the green leaves of the vineyard he pictures the delicious *escargots*, the snails, nibbling away. To Pierre, all the world is one big beautiful meal.

A car stops and the driver calls to Pierre, "I am a stranger to these parts. Can you tell me, young man, where I can find *La Bonne Vache*?"

Pierre leans into the car to give directions to his family's restaurant. On the seat next to the man he glimpses a paper that says "Inspection Form." On the form is the name of the famous company that awards stars to restaurants. If the restaurant is very, very, very good it receives a star and people from all over go there to eat. Inspectors test the restaurant by having a meal there, but there is a strict rule that the identity of the inspector must never be revealed.

Pierre gives directions to the inspector who thanks him and drives away.

Pierre pedals as fast as he can. Should he tell his mother and father who the inspector is? No. He could tell about the stranger coming to the restaurant, but it would not be honorable to tell who he is.

Out of breath he bursts into the kitchen. "Maman, Papa, a stranger is coming a long distance to eat at our restaurant!"

Monsieur Valcourt consults the reservations. "*Oui!* There is a name I don't recognize."

He slaps his forehead and declares, "With so little notice how are we to produce a meal worthy of someone who has come a long distance to eat at *La Bonne Vache? Impossible!*"

"I don't have any wild strawberries to make my famous *gâteau aux fraises. Impossible!*" says Pierre's mother.

Pierre recalls from his history class what the great General Napoléon said. He tells his parents, "*Impossible n'est pas français.*" Impossible is not French.

The mother, the father, and Pierre stand at attention. Together they repeat, "*Impossible n'est pas français.*"

"Pierre," his father says, "you must go into the village for us."

Pierre races on his bicycle to the village. When Pierre tells Madame Farcy, the *crémière*, of the special occasion she chooses a cheese so soft, so silken, and with such a subtle aroma, she weeps to part with it.

At the butcher shop Monsieur Camus selects, as he always does, a perfect cut of meat for the *boeuf à la mode*.

Monsieur Moreau picks out tiny onions like pearls, potatoes no larger than marbles, lettuces as tender as rose petals, and hands Pierre a basket of plump snails, but alas, he has no strawberries for Pierre's mother.

Madame Valcourt is close to tears. "My *gâteau* will be nothing without strawberries."

Pierre knows a place in the woods and hurries off with his basket.

Beneath the ferns is a patch of wild strawberries. Pierre gets on his knees and carefully plucks the tiny berries.

"What will we have for the fish course?" his father asks. "The cod that I planned to serve tonight comes from the ocean, miles away. I must have something from our own countryside for the guest."

"I'll get a trout for you, Papa."

Pierre catches a jar full of grasshoppers, takes up
his fishing pole, and hurries to the river. He knows
all the places where the trout hide: under the shade
of the branches that hang over the stream, in the
deep holes where the water is cool, in the little
riffles that catch the tasty insects.

A quarter hour goes by, a half hour, three quarters
of an hour. At last Pierre feels a tug on his line.
A fine trout.

On his way across the woods from the river a miracle occurs. Pierre sees the first *morilles* of the season. The rare mushrooms have a delicate perfume and give a magic to any dish. Carefully Pierre gathers the mushrooms.

"Look, Papa, what I have found for the *boeuf à la mode*."

"Very nice, Pierre, but not traditional," his papa says. "We must prepare our *boeuf à la mode* just as I have always prepared it and as your grandfather prepared it."

The regular guests are seated at their tables. Madame Brissac is there with her little dog, Miette. Monsieur Delage is having his customary *pouding au chocolat*. Madame Jupien and Monsieur Jupien, as they always do, are tasting each other's dinners.

In the kitchen the trout is shimmering in its coat of *gelée*. The lettuces are delicately dressed. The *boeuf à la mode* is simmering with its little potatoes and onions.

The cheese is relaxing and Pierre's mother is decorating the *gâteau* with the strawberries.

But Papa is unhappy. "I am the chef, but I am also the *patron*. At a great restaurant the *patron* is there to greet the guest. But I dare not leave the *boeuf à la mode* even for a moment and your mother is *très occupée*."

Pierre says, "Papa, I can watch the *boeuf à la mode*."

His father is about to say, "*Impossible.*" Instead he snatches off his *toque* and hurries away to don the striped trousers and dinner jacket of a *patron*.

Pierre stands on a chair and stirs, adjusting the fire so there are only little bubbles, and no big ones. On the kitchen table are the *morilles* with their delicate perfume.

While his mother's back is turned Pierre snatches the *morilles* and drops them into the *boeuf à la mode*.

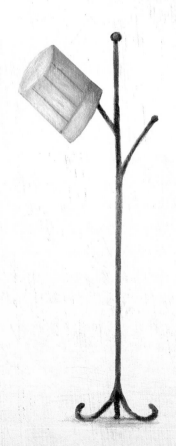

Moments later his father appears. He mops the perspiration from his face and replaces his *toque*. "The guest is here," he says, and snatching up the plate with the trout places it in the hands of the waiter, Albert. When Albert comes back the plate is empty.

But when the salad plate returns there is a tiny leaf no larger than a mouse's ear. Alas, the leaf is a bit wilted and has been rejected by the guest.

"A tragedy!" cries Pierre's mother.

As Pierre's father ladles out the *boeuf à la mode* he sees the *morilles*. His face turns red and then white. "*Quelle horreur!*" he shouts.

Pierre runs out the kitchen door.

When Pierre has the *courage* to creep back his father forgives him for the guest's plate with the *boeuf à la mode* has come back scraped clean, *morilles* and all!

"The guest has finished the *gâteau*," Papa says, "and is now having his *café*."

As the guest leaves *La Bonne Vache*, he summons Monsieur Valcourt and announces to the astounded *patron*, "I am not merely a guest, sir. I am an inspector from the company with the stars."

He thanks Monsieur Valcourt for the meal and departs.

Pierre's mother falls into a swoon. His father falls onto a chair. "Pierre," Monsieur Valcourt asks, "did you know our guest was an inspector?"

"Yes, Papa."

"Though we may never receive a star, Pierre, you were right to keep the secret. I would rather have a son who has *honneur* than a star for *La Bonne Vache*."

Two weeks go by with no word from the company with the stars. The wheat has ripened in the field. The raspberries have been picked. The plums have turned purple in the orchards and are ready to turn into a tart. At *La Bonne Vache* dinners are served but faces are long.

One morning Pierre looks out to see the postman approaching and behind him the entire village led by Madame Farcy, the *crémière*; Monsieur Moreau, the greengrocer; and Monsieur Camus, the butcher.

The postman hands Pierre's father a letter and on the envelope is the return address of the famous company with the stars. Everyone crowds around. They assure Pierre's family that it does not matter about the star. While they all know there is no better restaurant than *La Bonne Vache*, one can't expect a small village to compete with the great restaurants of Paris, though in truth, it would be a great *honneur* for the village.

The hands of Pierre's father tremble as he opens the envelope and takes out the letter. "We have awarded you a star," the letter says. When the letter speaks of the delicacy of the *gâteau*, Pierre's mother blushes with pleasure.

But the most complimentary words are saved for the *boeuf à la mode*. The inspector writes, "I was especially pleased to see the innovation of the *morilles*. Their delicate perfume added greatly to the traditional *boeuf à la mode*."

"Pierre," Papa says,
"now you may cook."

Afterword

You and I might grab a sandwich for lunch before hurrying off. It's not like that in France. Even young children are expected to sit down and take the time to ENJOY their meal. The preparation of a meal in France, whether in a home or a restaurant, is a challenge and an exciting occasion. Lunches can last two hours. In France food is important and not just the eating of it, but the shopping and preparation as well. Fine cooks don't just go to the supermarket once a week. They take their baskets and shop every day to get the freshest green bean or the most succulent tomato.

One of the most admired professions in France is that of the chef. The careers of famous chefs are followed in the newspapers as avidly as the lives of famous politicians or soccer players. A young boy like Pierre who wishes to cook can aspire to a fine career.

And there is indeed a company that awards stars to fine restaurants, but every meal someone prepares for you with love deserves a star.

Glossary

boeuf à la mode (bauf ah lah mode): a very special beef stew

café (kafe): coffee or coffee shop

courage (koo razh): courage

crémière/crémièr (kremjer): dairy-/cheese woman/man

escargots (es car go): snails, usually prepared with butter and garlic

gâteau aux fraises (gah to oh FREZ): cake with strawberries

gelée (zhe lay): jelly

honneur (aw neur): honor

impossible (EN paw seebl): impossible

impossible n'est pas français (EN paw seeble nay pas frahn SAY):
Impossible is not French

La Bonne Vache (la bawn vash): the good cow

morilles (mor ay): wild mushrooms

Oui (wee): yes

patron (pa TROHN): the owner of a restaurant

pouding au chocolat (poo ding oh shaw kaw la): chocolate pudding

Quelle horreur (kell or uhr): what a horror

soufflé (sue flay): a fluffy baked dish

toque (tawk): the traditional tall white hat worn by a chef

très occupée/occupé (tray aw ku PAY): very busy

DATE DUE

PRINTED IN U.S.A.